First U.S. edition 1992
The text and illustrations in this book first appeared in
Jack the Carpenter and His Friends, Jill the Farmer and Her Friends,
Tom the Greengrocer and His Friends, Julie the Paper Girl and Her Friends
all first published in Great Britain by
Walker Books Ltd., London in 1986.

ISBN 1-56402-056-8
Library of Congress Catalog Card Number 91-58719
Library of Congress Cataloging-in-Publication
information is available.

10 9 8 7 6 5 4 3 2 1
Printed and bound in Hong Kong by
Dai Nippon Printing Co.

The illustrations in this book are watercolor paintings

Candlewick Press
2067 Massachusetts Avenue
Cambridge, MA 02140

BUSY PEOPLE

by Nick Butterworth

CANDLEWICK PRESS
CAMBRIDGE, MASSACHUSETTS

Jack is a carpenter.

What does he use?

Anna is a doctor.

Why has she come?

Tom is a grocer.

What does he sell?

Bill is a repairman.

What does he fix?

Jenny is a gardener.

What does she use?

Steve is a fisherman.

What does he sail?

Betty is a baker.

What does she bake?

Jim is a messenger.

What does he ride?

Sally owns a clothing store.

What does she sell?

Dave is a builder.

What does he drive?

Ron has a hardware store.

What does he sell?

Jill is a farmer.

What does she drive?

Pete is a mechanic.

What does he use?

Fred is a garbage collector.

What does he pick up?